I0725977

FIST FIGHTER :

CODE OF HONOUR

Stephen Taylor

Published by

Dayglo Books Ltd, Nottingham, UK

www.dayglobooks.co.uk

0002-14-1920-13

Cover artwork & illustrations by
www.valentineart.co.uk

Typeset in Opendyslexic
by Abelardo Gonzales (2013)

Printed by IngramSpark

Distributed by Filament Publishing Ltd, Croydon

FIST FIGHTER :

CODE OF HONOUR

"Sammy, is that you Sammy?"

Samuel Medina started, looked around. The light was beginning to fail, but he perceived the merest presence of a figure in a doorway.

He hesitated for a moment, but the London streets were dangerous places. He turned and strode briskly away.

"Sammy! Don't go, Sammy! It's me," the voice called urgently.

Samuel stopped abruptly.

There was something about that voice.

"Who's there? Come out and show yourself, sir."

Resting its frame limply against the doorway, the shadowy figure now stood upright in response to Samuel's stern command.

"Show yourself, sir," Samuel said again, agitated now.

"It's me. Don't you know me, Sammy?" the figure shuffled out the shadows.

Samuel peered into the half-light. "My God!" he exclaimed, "it's John Campbell-John!"

"You remember me, then?"

"Oh, yes." Samuel took a step backwards. "I remember you all right; you don't forget a liar and a cheat. You don't forget embezzlement – you don't forget betrayal."

He worked his mouth and spat a gob of spittle onto the cobbles.

"Betrayal is an ugly word, Sammy boy."

Samuel's hands curled into fists.

"What would you call it, then?" he shot back.

"It was just self-preservation that's all. I went to ground for the sake of my health," Campbell-John shuffled his feet, grinned nervously.

"Your health!" exclaimed Samuel, his anger barely contained, the words sticking in his throat. "I have no time for this. It's the Sabbath, I need to get home."

He turned abruptly and walked away. He wanted nothing to do with the man.

Chapter 2   **A Visitor in the Night**

Later that evening, his wife and children long gone to their beds, Samuel sat by his fire and reflected.

A knocking at his door broke his concentration. He knew instinctively who it was.

The fire crackled. He stared into the dancing flames, ignoring the knock. But it persisted, growing in volume, until he could ignore it no longer.

Jumping up in alarm, he angrily pulled the door open, and recognised John Campbell-John.

"Be gone with you before you wake the neighbourhood!" he exclaimed.

He slammed the door shut and returned to his chair in front of the fire.

For a few moments all was quiet but then the knocking started again. This time it was accompanied by a muffled voice.

It was a voice that had fuelled anger within Samuel for fourteen long years. That anger had demanded revenge and retribution and taken many years to subside. Now it was back again, burning passionately within his breast.

"Be gone, I tell you," he yelled, the words tapering away when he realised he would awaken his family.

"Sammy boy, let me in. I need to talk to you."

"But why should I want to talk to you?"

"Because," said John Campbell-John, but then he paused, as though he could not find a creditable reason.

"Because you were the best friend I ever had, and I treated you grievously."

Samuel was in turmoil, but slowly he opened the door. He could not have explained why.

"You had better come in and sit down."

Gazing intently at his visitor, Samuel thought how pathetic the man looked – considerably older than his five and forty years. Despite himself, Samuel found much of his anger had drained away.

He indicated a chair and fetched two tankards of ale. They drank slowly, in silence, staring into the flames.

"Have you come to pay me back, then?" Samuel asked at length.

"If only I could Sammy boy," said John, "but the money was all gone a long time ago."

"Now, why doesn't that surprise me?"

A smile crossed John's lips.

Samuel noticed it and for some reason smiled too, though he knew not why.

There was a shared memory, a joint recollection, triggered by that phrase. They knew each other so well. They had shared so much together.

"Why now?" asked Samuel. "You haven't come looking for money have you? Because if you have, you'll get none here."

"No Sammy, I haven't come to take money from you. I could tell you lies and say I'm rich, I'm doing well, but it's obvious the last few years have not been kind to me. In fact, I didn't seek you out at all. I saw you merely by chance and I slipped into a doorway so I could observe you.

"But then I just couldn't resist speaking to you. I thought you looked well – you looked prosperous. I was pleased. I found myself happy to see you."

"And what," asked Samuel, "do you come to offer me by way of reparation?"

"I can offer you nothing – except to build some bridges – if you'll let me."

"And how do you propose to do that?"

"I don't know, Sammy."

"I haven't been called that for fifteen years," Samuel mumbled quietly, adding in a fierce whisper, "I ought to thrash you."

He looked intently at John, who met his eye and smiled back affectionately.

"Aye, that was always your first instinct, wasn't it?" John smiled knowingly.

"And the thought did cross my mind before I spoke to you," he added.

"But you spoke to me anyway?"

"Aye. I thought it worth a good thrashing – to speak to you again."

Samuel reflected on those words for a time. He sat staring into the fire.

"So, what now, then?

"Perhaps we can reminisce," John shrugged. "We had so many good times, didn't we?"

"Yes, we did, didn't we?" Samuel's face lit up as he broke into a laugh. "We did that, right enough."

"We did more than that Sammy boy," said John excitedly. "We changed the world, didn't we? You were the most famous man in England. You couldn't go anywhere without being required to present yourself to the public.

"Three huzzahs – all the time three huzzahs they gave you – from the lowest to the highest in the land."

"Aye, even the Prince of Wales himself."

"I still don't know how you managed to keep winning – you were by rights much too small, you know. How did you do it, Sammy boy?"

"I mastered my art, John. You fight on your own terms not your opponent's."

"Aye, and you were never short on confidence were you? You could be an arrogant so and so."

Samuel emptied his tankard, slapped it down with a grin, "Yes I was – it's true. I thought I could beat the world; that nothing could stop me."

John gave a chuckle, "And we spent so much money didn't we, Sammy – we lived liked princes though, didn't we?"

"Oh, yes, we did that right enough. But perhaps, if you'd paid your dues along the way, things may have turned out differently."

"Aye, so many regrets, Sammy boy, so many regrets. But so many great memories as well."

"Aye, I suppose so."

The two men fell silent. Suddenly Samuel smiled, "Do you remember when we first met?"

"Oh I do. I remember it well, Sammy boy. A spring morning in 1785 and a brash young Jewish boy wanting to fight the world . . ."

CHAPTER 3   **The Squire's Son**

In 1785 Captain John Campbell-John cut a fine figure of a man. He wore the uniform of an infantry captain, which complemented his fine physique and good looks.

He strode with full military style. His shoulders were square, accentuating every inch of his tall, five-feet-eleven-inches frame.

His blonde hair escaped and flowed from the back of his shako.

He was the quintessential military second son of an English country gentleman.

Except, in truth, he was none of these.

John Campbell-John was not his real name. He was not a captain. Nor was he the son of a country gentleman – that is to say, not the legitimate son.

He was born to an intelligent, pretty, but naïve governess who had been employed to educate the Squire's children, a task she was rather good at.

So much so, that when she became pregnant by the Squire, rather than lose her he arranged for her to marry his bailiff.

For many years afterwards, the Squire continued to enjoy the best of all worlds. He had a first class governess, well-educated children, and a mistress at his beck and call whenever his fancy turned to thoughts of an ardent nature.

Added to this, the lady of the house turned a blind eye to the whole affair. It seemed that everyone was happy – with the possible exception of the bailiff, one Campbell John.

But he was only too well aware of his place as a servant and knew better than to complain. So he kept his feelings to himself and got on with his job.

Into this unorthodox, but by no means unique world, was born to the governess a son. The child was accepted by Campbell John as his own son and was christened Edward John.

The master of the house had also fathered two legitimate sons.

The first, similarly called Edward, was five years old when John entered this world. The second son, George, preceded him by only a matter of four months.

As the boys grew up they were allowed to play together, and John was accepted about the big house. The Squire took a shine to him and indulged him, much to the annoyance of his wife.

John was everything George was not.

He was outgoing, where George was timid. He was entertaining, where George was a bit dour. He was rugged, where George was scrawny.

The problem for the Squire was that John was everything he wanted in a son, whereas poor George was a bit of a disappointment. The Squire saw in young John a chip off the old block. Every day, watching the boys play, he was reminded of this fact – John even looked like him.

As the boys grew they got into more and more mischief and it was John who was the main perpetrator. But he always had enough nous to taint George with his roguery.

He had the ability to get away with his mischief purely by the force of his personality. He would look at his natural father with a twinkle in his eye and the Squire's stern face would switch uncontrollably to a smile.

Though John could do no wrong in the Squire's eyes, his stepmother grew to hate him.

When John was nineteen, the Squire died.

He had promised to look after John in his will, but Edward inherited everything. He soon found an excuse to rid himself of his half-brother.

John was sent on his way with five guineas, a horse, and a change of clothes, and was expected to be thankful for that.

He had no trade and only his wits to sustain him.

He had been sheltered from any sense of responsibility in his youth. Consequently, within days he was penniless and forced to sell his horse. Within days of that he was again penniless.

And so he turned to soldiery. He joined an infantry regiment as a common foot soldier. To his amazement, he loved it.

There were many hours of boredom in the soldier's life. John was just the man to fill this vacuum. It gave him endless scope for his gambling, wenching and pranks.

This period in his life, however, added guile and worldliness to his array of talents. It was a secondary education. John was learning how to con his way through life – honest toil was not the route for him.

And then, on one drunken evening a plot was hatched and a bet was proposed. The officers of his company had been invited to a country ball, along with officers from the rest of the regiment. The bet was that John should go and pass himself off as an officer.

Impersonating an officer was a very serious offence. However, even after sobering up, the notion took hold of him.

He had the education, the accent, the knowledge of the 'big house'. He decided he would do it. A bribe was made to a laundry wench and an officer's uniform obtained.

The success of the venture astounded even him. He was accepted totally. Even officers from his own company, who had many times put him on a charge, failed to recognise him.

Officers never really looked enlisted men in the eye – but it was much more than that. John learned that evening that people see what is in front of them – image is all-important. A life lesson had been learned.

Sometime afterwards, on this fine spring morning John strode purposefully down a London street. It was his first time in the capital.

Buoyed by his successes at impersonating an officer, he had deserted his regiment and invented the persona of "John Campbell-John".

His intention was to con his way through the city – to make his fortune. He had thought little further than that. No detailed plan had evolved in his mind.

Today, however, John Campbell-John was to hit the jackpot at his first attempt.

His perambulations took him towards Smithfield Market, known locally as Ruffians Hall. But then he turned and looked up an adjacent street, and became aware of a fracas. He moved towards it, drawn somehow to what was happening.

An impromptu ring was being formed outside a greengrocer's establishment. A fight was about to take place but the two adversaries seemed to be totally mismatched. The first was a stout, athletic man in the prime of his life, standing nearly six feet tall.

His adversary was a youth of eighteen or nineteen years of age, standing no more than five feet eight inches. He had removed his shirt and stood ready to fight wearing only his breeches and a pair of yarn stockings. His thighs were powerful and his upper body lean, but even so, John could see only a mismatch.

Throughout the crowd, odds were being given as to the outcome. Three to one against the youth seemed to John very poor odds as he had neither the strength nor the size to best his competitor – surely, he thought, ten to one would be more realistic.

And yet there were some takers. John could not have passed this opportunity by even had he wanted to. The temptation was irresistible. A design registered in his mind.

Here was the prospect of funds, an opportunity for advancement. It was an irrational thought. This was no more than a street fight and they happened all the time. Yet his instincts told him he was right.

With an engaging smile, he moved over to address the underdog. "What occasion brings you to this fight, youth?"

"I am apprenticed to these greengrocer's premises, sir, and this fellow has insulted my mistress on account of her being of the Jewish religion," said the young man.

"And is this your fight, lad?"

"It is, sir. When my master remonstrated with the fellow for his impropriety, he became more abusive and challenged him to a fight."

"So it's not really your fight, is it?" said John, taken aback by the youth's educated speech.

"My master is not a young and athletic man, sir. The man is a bully and I intend to punish him for his insolence."

"You have an eloquent tongue to match your bravery, young man, but I fear your resolve is foolhardy. You have neither the size nor the strength for this fight. Let me broker a truce on your behalf."

"Thank you, sir, for your benevolence, but I beg leave to embrace this challenge. I may not have the size or the strength, but I have the science to best this man," the youth asserted.

"You have an education, that is clear, and if your fighting is as fancy as your words then we may yet all be surprised. Do you have a second for this set-to, and if not, then may I offer my services?"

"No, sir, I do not have a second, and I will gladly accept your services."

"Then let us get to it," said John.

What followed was a revelation to the crowd and especially to John Campbell-John. He had witnessed several set-tos in the army. They were usually brutal affairs, the conqueror being the biggest and strongest fellow.

But this lad had an athleticism that counteracted and nullified the strength of his opponent.

For the first five minutes of the contest the youth advanced and retreated so that his opponent's punches fell short, or were parried. As the other man tired, his shots became increasingly wild and easier to evade, all the time draining his stamina and strength.

After twelve minutes the youth changed his tactics and began to attack, advancing and landing clean shots and then retreating before the ponderous blows of his antagonist could connect. After seventeen minutes his challenger was bloodied and exhausted, while the youth had not a mark on him.

A solid blow to the ribs sent the bigger man to the ground gasping for air, and he had to be revived by his second before being sent out to fight again. This happened four more times until his opponent was no longer able to stand, and cried, "Bested!"

The crowd had swelled enormously during the fight, many having been drawn from Ruffians Hall. It included a sporting-looking gentleman who had taken immense pleasure in the performance of the youth. John doffed his shako and went for the opportunity.

"Nubbins, sirs!" he cried and thrust his cap before them, "let us all show our appreciation!"

With that he produced his last sovereign from his tunic tossed it into his cap and thrust the cap before the gentleman. It had the desired effect. A bright golden guinea was plucked from a silk waistcoat.

"Bravo to the lad!" cried the sporting gentleman. Other coins followed, as John persuaded the assembled crowd who were now keen to pat the youth on his shoulders.

"Bravo!" now cried the throng in unison, enthralled by the lad's display. The coins began to flow more rapidly and John needed both hands to support the weight of his cap as he carried it over to the victor.

"There's a tidy collection here for you, lad. Where shall we go to count it?"

"The Boar tavern sir," said the youth, "but give my opponent a guinea for his sport today."

"Well said, lad," one of the sporting gentlemen remarked, "we've all had good sport here today."

"Two tankards of ale, landlord," said John, "and do you have a place where my good friend and I can discuss a little business?"

"Been fighting again, young Samuel?" The landlord shook his head at Samuel.

"Aye sir, but it was not to be avoided."

"It never is with you, lad, is it?" The landlord winked pointedly at John and showed the pair to a cubicle.

As they sat down, John thrust out his hand. "John Campbell-John, and to whom do I have the honour this fine day?"

"Samuel Medina, your servant, sir."

"You have fine manners for a working lad, Samuel Medina."

"Thank you, sir. I was educated at a Jewish school and have some learning."

"And you have some fighting ability, too, lad."

"Yes, sir – I was never bested at school."

"But that was no child you have just beaten, Samuel lad. Where did you learn to fight like that?"

John Campbell-John saw something in this young man. Something special. Something he could exploit. John was not motivated by anything noble, merely his instinct to make the most of this situation.

Supping his ale, Samuel surreptitiously eyed the young soldier across the table and wondered why he was being so kind. It had been good of him to collect a purse for the fight, but Samuel, naturally suspicious of strangers, was not sure how much to trust him.

But there was another side to Samuel. He was an extrovert. He loved the limelight and he had one special talent that gave him the attention he craved. He could fight. It wasn't that he was quarrelsome. In fact, he had quite a sunny and genuine nature.

It was that he liked to show off. He justified the need to fight by convincing himself that these were noble actions. He would come to the rescue of anybody, whether they needed it or not.

It was a sad fact of life that Jew-baiting was a popular sport in London. Any Jew was liable to be assailed in the street. Passers-by did not interfere any more than did the law.

But the young Jews of Samuel's generation were no longer prepared to stand for this baiting and had begun to fight back.

Most fought out of necessity, in self-defence, but Samuel did it out of – well, not so much the pleasure of the fight, but of being in the limelight.

He knew he was an attention seeker – his friends were always telling him so. At the first signs of an insult to himself or someone else, he would challenge the perpetrator to withdraw his words – to apologise or be thrashed for their insolence.

The result was that in his post-school life he was fighting increasingly frequently. But now his opponents were usually bigger and stronger than he.

He developed a science of the pugilistic art that was all his own, to the point where none in the locality could stand against him. And he was just a boy of nineteen.

"So come on, lad, tell me where you are from and where you learned to fight like that."

"From Bethnal Green and I am self-taught, sir."

"And how much have you earned from your fighting, lad?"

Samuel looked down at a stain on the table.

"Why, I have never earned anything before, sir."

"Nothing?" John was amazed. "So how much do you think we have here?"

"I don't know."

"Well, let's count it, shall we?" John emptied his shako onto the table.

"Five pounds, twelve shillings and seven pence." He counted the coins into neat piles.

"And a sovereign, sir." Samuel looked wide-eyed across the table. John looked down, shook his head.

"I think not. We have counted together – there is no mistake."

"But you took out a sovereign as we crossed the road to this tavern, sir."

"You have a suspicious nature, young Samuel."

"That's as may be, but I will not be cheated."

"Cheated? I'm not here to cheat you, lad."

"Then put back the sovereign you took." Samuel stood up, and fixed John with a stern gaze. "If not, sir, I fear we have to go outside to settle this."

Discomfited, John shifted his position on the bench.

He looked up and met Samuel's gaze. The lad had large brown eyes that were warm and compassionate.

He wore his hair in a pigtail, and his face was clean-shaven. His general countenance reflected his kind-heartedness. His olive skin and aquiline nose were softened by those two great soulful eyes.

Now, however, all trace of compassion had left Samuel's features.

Hiding a qualm of disquiet, John Campbell-John sat back and looked at him intently. He had thought the lad would be easy to manipulate, but now he saw that Samuel was no fool.

Those large brown eyes penetrated back into his consciousness. He perceived that the lad's challenge was serious and he had the resolve to back it up. John sensed within himself a scintilla of fear.

Fear was not something he was familiar with. He had lived a life virtually without restraint. He had always done whatever he wanted and to hell with the cost. Now, suddenly, he was faced with consequences – immediate consequences.

He knew he could not best the lad in a fist-fight. With that thought, his cunning took over.

"Aye lad, you're right, I did remove a sovereign," said John, deciding that discretion was called for.

"But I was not trying to cheat you. It was merely the float. To take up a collection you have to get it started, to get those sporting gentlemen to dip into their pockets.

"I am not in the best of funds at the moment and I haven't got a sovereign to spare."

Samuel looked at him calmly.

"Nevertheless, sir, your sovereign was put in my

collection. By my reckoning that makes it mine."

"Very well, Samuel Medina, your point is well made." John plucked the sovereign from his tunic and threw it on the pile of money before them.

Samuel's features softened and a smile crossed his lips as he resumed his seat. John returned his smile, but it was more forced than natural.

"I am a generous man though, John Campbell-John," said Samuel to John's surprise, "and I am obliged to you for taking up a collection for me. You can take a guinea from it for your trouble."

"You are a strange man, Samuel Medina," said John. "You would fight me for a sovereign and now you give me a guinea."

"Aye, maybe I am, but you should know that I am not to be cheated," said Samuel, "and neither am I a fool."

"No, you're not that, Sammy lad." John rolled the coin in his fingers. "In fact, I see prosperity for both of us. I envisage a great partnership if you are interested. How say you?"

"I am interested in bettering myself, sir."

"I promise you, Sammy lad, that money is the quickest way of bettering yourself. If you can become a man of property then many doors will open for you."

"What is your part in this partnership to be?"

"I'll be your second and your manager. I'll arrange the fights and negotiate the purse. I'll find you a patron to back you and we'll have great adventures along the way."

"What will your cut be for these services?"

"Fifty/fifty, Sammy lad. What do you say?"

Samuel grimaced.

"Seventy-five/twenty-five is more equitable."

"Sixty/forty," said John.

"Seventy-five/twenty-five," Samuel repeated.

John thought for a moment.

"Very well, Sammy lad, then we have a deal."

                    The Light of Israel

In the next two years, the partnership prospered.

On a hot summer's day, they had their first professional fight before a large crowd at Marylebone Fields. The main attraction was a bout between the people's favourite, Big Charles Sweep, and Norbert Openshaw, 'The Lancashire Soldier'.

The first supporting battle was between Irish Michael the Carrier and Samuel the Jew, or 'The Light of Israel', as he insisted on calling himself.

Irish Michael the Carrier seemed the ideal choice. He was a man of thirty-eight, a veteran of many pitched battles. He bore the marks of his trade with pride.

His face was riddled with scar tissue stretched tight over his angular bone structure. He had cauliflower ears that protruded like a pair of wing nuts.

He was, by profession, a sedan chair carrier. That had contributed to his immense strength. He was also a tall man, standing five feet eleven and with a long reach in proportion to his size.

He had retained that strength, but his weight had now risen to sixteen and a half stone, much of which was being carried around his ample middle.

He would have a height advantage of three inches over Samuel, and a weight advantage of five stones – it would look to the crowd like a mismatch.

John Campbell-John saw this as an opportunity, and got odds of five-to-one against Samuel from the bookmakers. He gambled everything they had.

The Irishman was used to standing toe to toe with his opponent, using his strength and parrying skills. However, Samuel made him chase him around the ring.

He easily beat the aging man, who was exhausted after only twelve minutes. Their gambling winnings were far more than the five guineas purse for the fight.

Successive fights went the same way, John Campbell-John matching Samuel in a series of fights against men he seemed to be too small to best. Each time he did so, his fame spread.

He was making a name for himself. He was being written about in newspapers and boxing magazines.

Chapter 8   A Fight on the Sabbath

John's cunning now changed tack. He sought and found a sponsor.

Sir Thomas Kettall was the youngest son of the Duke of Howden and a well-known sporting gentleman.

John wanted Samuel to get fights at the prestigious Fives Court, before the wealthy sporting gentlemen. Kettall duly obliged and a meeting was arranged to discuss the fight and Samuel's opponent.

"A tough fight, Medina. Against Daniel the Gravedigger. Have you seen him fight? Can you best him?" Kettall asked.

"The Bristol Bonecrusher? Yes, I've seen him fight. He's fit and strong, and he likes to wrestle, but I can best him."

"Glad to hear it," said Kettall, "then it's at the Fives Court, the first Saturday of next month. I'll see you there."

"Oh, no, you won't," said Samuel.

"What!" Kettall swung round in astonishment.

"I don't fight on the Sabbath," said Samuel.

Exasperated, Kettall snapped, "But it's not the damned Sabbath."

"I am a follower of Judaism, sir – it is my Sabbath."

"Nonsense," said Kettall, "it's all arranged, and that is an end to it."

Samuel puffed out his chest.

"It is not an end to it, sir," he said. "I shall not fight – you must get somebody else."

"You will fight, Medina, and on the first Saturday of next month, or I'll be damned if I won't make sure you never fight again."

"Then you must do your worst, sir, for I will not fight on the Sabbath," said Samuel. "And that *is* an end to it."

Kettall blustered and waved his arms. "You talk some sense into him, Campbell-John," he bawled, as he walked away.

John looked long and hard at Samuel without speaking, but his expression spoke volumes. It said: 'dunderhead'.

Samuel read the unspoken word and understood the disappointment conveyed by John's expression. But he failed to read his friend's desperation.

John was broke, despite the enormous sums he had earned from Samuel's fighting.

He had suffered huge losses at the card table. Worse, he was in debt and he had no income to finance his lifestyle, let alone to pay off his creditors.

Samuel's next fight was to have been his passage out of this predicament.

"Don't look at me like that," said Samuel, "this time it's different."

"It always is."

"But this is my religion."

"It's always something or the other."

"Maybe, maybe," said Samuel, "but you have always known that I will not fight on the Sabbath."

"Sometimes it's necessary to bend before the wind, you know," said John, peevishly.

Samuel did not reply.

"But oh, no, not you. You'd stand tall against the worst tempest," John grumbled.

"But it's not right to fight on the Sabbath."

"This is London, Sammy. It doesn't stop for the Jewish Sabbath. Sometimes things are unavoidable."

"So I must compromise my beliefs so that someone else can make money, that's the size of it."

"You are a name now, Samuel – a big draw. I can get you big fights, but those fights come with conditions. I can get you a fine purse and I have – one hundred guineas. But the fight has to be on a Saturday."

"Then we have a problem, for I will not fight on a Saturday and nothing you can say or do will make me change my mind."

The noise from the packed terraces of the Fives Court was frenzied. It signalled the expectation of the crowd to the combatants.

The two antagonists, locked away in their changing rooms, could not escape the anticipation that was evident all around them.

In these circumstances Samuel was usually calm, for he was abnormally confident in his own abilities. He was brave, but in some respects his bravery was blind. It was a kind of deliberate blindness, for he knew that pugilists could be maimed for life, or even killed in the course of these pitched battles.

They were called pitched battles because a fight would continue for as long as it took, until one man was bested – beaten to the point where he could no longer go on.

Today, however, Samuel was anxious. He was not afraid of The Bristol Bonecrusher. What he feared was something much worse than a fellow pugilist.

He feared that God would desert him, for he had succumbed to pressure and agreed to fight on the Sabbath.

He fought under the banner of 'The Light of Israel', and he believed this pleased his God. He believed, conversely, that fighting on the Sabbath would anger Him.

Samuel sat on a bench and attended to the routine that he always adopted before any fight.

He was oiling his upper torso when John and

Kettall arrived. He did not stop what he was doing.

"We can't get better than six-to-four on," said John, "it's two-to-one against the Gravedigger."

"It was bound to happen," said Samuel arrogantly, "my reputation now goes before me."

"Aye it does," said Kettall agreeably. "They have come to see you today, Samuel Medina, much more than the Gravedigger."

"Then I will give them the display they have come to see," said Samuel, adding, "God willing, of course."

"You haven't needed God's help before," said John suspiciously.

He had noticed the tone of caution in Samuel's voice.

"I always take my God into the ring with me," said Samuel, "my skills come as a gift from Him."

"Then it is time to display those God-given skills, Sammy lad."

"Aye, and will you wager twenty-five guineas for me, John? I will take six-to-four on."

These words reinforced John's confidence in Samuel. He would take, as his percentage cut, twenty-five guineas from Samuel's purse, but he needed more than that to pay off his creditors. He needed the gambling winnings.

Despite the genuine bond he had developed with Samuel over the last two years, money and debt were powerful forces in John's life. This was a silver-tongued scallywag of a man.

At heart he was not a man of high principles. He now just needed money. Although his friendship with Samuel demanded his loyalty, that loyalty was now second to this need.

Samuel came to the ring with the cheering of the crowd sounding in his ears. He was no longer the unknown Jew who could fight a bit. He was a hero.

Pugilists were men who embodied the virtues of what it was to be English – men who would stand up for what they believed to be right and who followed a noble pastime.

They reflected what their contemporaries saw as a sort of humanity – a man's right to stand and fight for what was his.

Because of his size, he seemed to reinforce the view that if your cause was just then it did not matter that your opponent was bigger and more powerful, for the English fighting spirit would see you succeed.

Samuel embodied this perception and yet he was a Jew. A Jew was not supposed to be part of this English perspective and yet paradoxically he had become the personification of it.

He was introduced to the crowd as Samuel the Jew, 'The Light of Israel'. The crowd cheered joyously, irrespective of the fact that many of them would return to Jew-baiting the following day.

He danced in a circle with his hands held high as his name was barked to the crowd. He played with their emotions like the most skilled of actors.

The Bristol Bonecrusher was also well known to the crowd, and was favoured for his bravery and defiance. He was a man with a reputation for not being easily beaten.

Today, however, he brought forth only the cheers of his own close friends and the subdued appreciation of the sporting gentlemen in the crowd.

In terms of size there was an advantage to the Gravedigger, but he was not a giant of a man. He was only two inches taller than Samuel. But his upper body was exceptionally well developed from his years working in the graveyard. His weight advantage was only about a stone and a half, for Samuel himself had filled out and his twenty-one-year-old frame was now more thickset than before.

The Gravedigger was red-haired and his skin was pale. This distracted from his physique, whereas Samuel was eye-catching in his physical splendour. His dark, oiled skin glowed and his muscles rippled in the light.

The overall impression was of an athlete, rather than a muscle-bound hulk.

The bell sounded and Samuel took up his fighting pose, his left leg and left arm extended.

The Gravedigger waded forward and threw heavy punches in a wide arc that Samuel easily evaded. Then Samuel responded by snapping his left fist into the man's face three times in rapid succession, so that his head jerked backwards like a buoy bobbing in the ocean.

After ten minutes the Gravedigger was heavily bloodied around the face whilst Samuel was unmarked.

When he saw that his opponent was beginning to slow, Samuel planted his feet, giving him the purchase to land more powerful punches. He sidestepped to the left of another wild punch. Then he placed his heels on the canvas and delivered a powerful right uppercut that sent the Gravedigger's head rocking backwards even more violently.

A spray of sweat took to the air like a flock of frightened birds. The crowd roared their approval.

The Gravedigger was stunned for a moment but Samuel did not follow up the attack, preferring to circle his opponent.

He raised his arms above his head to emphasise the power of the blow. The knowledgeable crowd needed little encouragement to cheer their hero a second time. Samuel loved to play to the crowd, but such lack of respect for his opponent was a dangerous strategy.

His senses having cleared, the Gravedigger came forward again. Now he decided upon a change of tactics.

He threw no more wild punches – in fact, he threw no more punches at all.

Samuel sidestepped to his left, but this time the Gravedigger merely reeled to his right in pursuit. Samuel repeated the sidestep but again the Gravedigger lurched to his right. Samuel changed tack and sidestepped to his right, but this time his opponent countered by moving to his left. Samuel's retreat was being cut off and he was being manoeuvred into a corner.

The Gravedigger then moved in, his legs in a wide stance. He swayed from side to side so that he could oppose any sideways move from Samuel.

However, the man still did not attempt to throw any punches. As he closed in, he put his open hands on Samuel's shoulder. His grip dug into his flesh, the thumbs digging deep into his neck. Samuel felt the pain penetrate his consciousness.

The Gravedigger was adept at wrestling as well as fist fighting, and he saw this now as his best chance of success. Samuel was aware that he would not win a wrestling match against this man. He had to escape.

He thrust his arms upwards inside those of the Gravedigger and then violently pulled them apart, forcing his opponent's grip to be broken.

He then brought his hands down and, with his fists clenched, punched his opponent strongly on the ears. Immediately he sidestepped away and raised his hands again to the crowd so that they could salute him. The Gravedigger was left with his ears ringing.

The man did not lack for courage, however. He came forward again. He was shaking his head repeatedly in an effort to clear the buzzing in his head.

Samuel was determined he was not going to allow himself to be caught in a corner again. He knew he had young, fresh legs to outpace his opponent, and this was allied to greater speed and agility.

He increased his tempo, and the Gravedigger seemed to have no answer to this. For the next ten minutes Samuel danced and flicked punch after punch into the reddened, bloodied face that was now chasing him incessantly, until he felt that the man's resolve was beginning to evaporate.

A lack of success can have a devastating effect on the mind – this was the Bonecrusher's dilemma.

Samuel saw this, and his movements now merged into a perfect harmony – feet, body, arms, and brain in total synchronisation. He was determined to put the Gravedigger away, as he appeared to be all but expended.

At twenty-four minutes into the fight, the Gravedigger trundled forward, and Samuel planted his feet with no attempt to sidestep the lunge.

He met his man head on, and let fly with

a wicked left hook and followed it with a right uppercut. The power of both punches was doubled because the man had walked onto them.

The Gravedigger sank to his knees, but the man's pride was stung. Immediately and surprisingly, he got to his feet.

His seconds called for the agreed thirty seconds time out under the rules, but their own fighter ignored them. He lunged forward again belligerently, and the referee waved the fight on.

The Gravedigger was a proud man. He was being beaten, and beaten easily, and to his perception this young upstart was ridiculing him.

But he led with his chin and it appeared to Samuel like an archery target. So Samuel obliged with another powerful upper cut, stopping his opponent in his tracks.

Samuel saw the man's eyes blur as his senses were addled and temporarily detached from his rational mind.

His opponent was a beaten man and ready to be despatched. He was now helpless before him.

Samuel raised his right hand high into the sky so that the crowd could witness his moment of triumph – he was playing to them.

The last punch would be with their lavish approval. It would be a spectacle. It would feed that part of him that was a showman.

It was not to be, however.

The Gravedigger's seconds dived into the ring. They grabbed Samuel's arm and restrained him, claiming that their man was entitled to the thirty-second time out to recover.

They knew that if this final blow landed, their

man would face inevitable defeat and not even thirty seconds of respite would counter that.

Pandemonium broke out. The ring was invaded from all sides. The melee continued for several minutes.

All this time Samuel was being held down and manoeuvred away from his seconds.

Then someone grabbed the hair at the nape of Samuel's neck so that his head was pulled back, forcing his vision skywards. His eyes protruded and gaped, brilliant with fear.

A piercing pain enveloped his lower back. It was the Gravedigger sinking punches into him. He was intent on taking advantage of the situation, inflicting as much damage as he could, although it was unclear whether this was pre-planned or just opportunistic.

Samuel cried out to John Campbell-John to help him but his cries were lost in the fracas.

The strength was draining from him with every blow, and he would have sunk to his knees but for the men restraining him. Then he lost consciousness.

Realising what damage they had done, the men released him. When he hit the floor the trampling crowd inflicted more damage, because his natural reflexes to protect himself were reduced to nothing by his unconsciousness.

John Campbell-John looked around the ring, panic taking him like a bolt of lightning out of a menacing sky.

He could not see Samuel and he was horror-struck. Eventually he managed to engage the help of a group of four men to make a human wedge and focussed it in the direction of the far corner.

They heaved and tugged and pushed, and the crowd ebbed and swayed before them. At last they began to make progress until they inched, step by resistant step, across the ring.

When they arrived they found Samuel slumped, still unconscious, his lips blue because of the lack of oxygen. A cage of legs imprisoned him.

They hauled him to his feet, frantically shouting at the crowd to give their man air, but nobody listened.

John held Samuel upright with the aid of the ropes, whilst the four other men formed a barricade around them.

Slowly, Samuel began to recover consciousness, but he was in a bad way.

It took more than twenty minutes for the ring to be cleared and John held Samuel all that time.

There was little sign that his friend had recovered sufficiently to take his own weight.

When the ring finally emptied they took him back to the corner and sat him down and tried to revive him with smelling salts.

They drenched him endlessly with a torrent of water and whirled towels frantically in an effort to increase his oxygen intake.

John examined Samuel's body and saw the bruising that had already begun to appear on his lower back. He knew all was not well.

"What have they done to you, Sammy lad?"

Samuel looked upwards at John, his large, dark eyes registering comprehension for the first time.

But that defiant spark had been extinguished so that they looked like the eyes of a beaten pup.

"They've done for my kidneys," he said, his voice only just audible.

"This is an outrageous foul," yelled John. "We'll claim a foul and take the purse."

At that moment the purse was the farthest thing from Samuel's fevered mind, but money was still a powerful force upon John.

Sir Thomas Kettall had been appointed as Samuel's umpire to act in the event of a dispute. John called him over and instructed him to claim the fight on a foul. Kettall agreed to speak with the Gravedigger's nominated umpire.

It was the custom to choose gentlemen of rank to act impartially for this task. Nevertheless John expected the two umpires would disagree and each stand up for their own man.

But then the Master of Ceremonies took to the stage and raised his hands for quiet.

"Gentlemen," he pronounced, "both the contestants have cried foul and have claimed the victory. The umpires have come to an understanding therefore.

Daniel the Gravedigger will accept the forfeit of his thirty seconds time out and Samuel the Jew will accept the interference from the Gravedigger's seconds. The fight will recommence."

John listened with stunned disbelief. Kettall, standing as Samuel's nominated umpire, had just handed the contest to the Gravedigger.

"The bastard must have bet against us, Sammy lad," said John with resignation. "Can you fight on?"

"I fear I cannot," said Samuel, "my strength has been beaten from me."

John signalled Kettall over and he arrived, shamelessly, without any visible sign of remorse.

"Our man is not fit to fight," said John, "why have you agreed for the fight to go on?"

"Both men have claimed foul," said Kettall, "and since Medina committed the first foul, it was the only solution for a sporting gentleman."

"You've bet on the Gravedigger haven't you?"

"You are impudent, sir," said Kettall evasively. "Mind your manners and remember how much you need my support. You'll be back playing cards for farthings without me standing as surety for you."

John dropped his head to hide his shame, for he knew that Samuel was being badly wronged. He had to do something but he knew not what.

"But Samuel is our man, is he not?" he said, attempting to sound contrite.

"Aye he is," said Kettall, "the Bonecrusher was at the point of defeat and should easily be bested again."

"But Samuel is unable to fight, we can't send him out again," said John pleadingly.

"Nonsense," said Kettall dismissively, "our man is a pugilist, and that's what they do. They fight until one man is bested. Medina knows the rules of engagement – he understands that."

"Aye, I do," said Samuel, stirring his wounded and painful body, "it is my duty to fight on."

Samuel put his right arm on the ropes and painfully hauled himself to his feet. His left hand held his side to ease the pain. Surprisingly, his legs held his weight and he turned to John."

"I don't want you to throw in the towel," he said, "you must let me decide if I'm beaten."

"You're a beaten man now, Samuel Medina," said John, "there's no more fight left in you. You're done for, lad."

"We'll see," said Samuel bravely. "Now, let us prepare to fight on."

Samuel and John were called to the square in the centre of the ring by the referee in preparation for the fight to recommence.

Samuel looked at the Gravedigger and tried to hide the pain he was feeling. The blood had been cleared away from the Gravedigger's face but it had been further mutilated.

It was misshapen with bumps and bruising and his right eye was almost closed.

Nevertheless, one good eye looked back at Samuel and indicated the man's intent. It said he knew he was about to win. He knew what damage he had already inflicted.

The bell sounded and Samuel eased his way forward. He turned his stance around to lead with his right hand, keeping his left to protect his side.

He flicked out a right into the Gravedigger's face but even that caused him pain. His opponent merely walked through the punch, making no attempt to throw punches back.

His objective was to cut off Samuel's retreat and back him into a corner. Samuel could see this, but his mobility was so restricted that he had difficulty in countering his adversary.

He tried to dance and flick out punches, but the man just kept walking through everything he threw. He felt the ropes on his back with nowhere to go.

He was trapped.

The Gravedigger leered at him as he pounced. He grabbed Samuel by the shoulders forcing him down-wards, but then released his grip and grabbed him by the hair again.

At the same time he started to punch, but those punches were directed at just one area – his back, and his kidneys in particular. Blow after blow sank into Samuel, but he was unable to free himself or respond.

John cried foul but there was nothing in the rules that said the Gravedigger could not do this – the kidneys were not out of bounds.

The holding of hair was not considered as manly and the crowd bayed its disapproval. It was not part of that perceived noble pursuit that pugilists personified, but the blows continued.

Samuel sank to his knees but was hauled up and held by his opponent, who then continued to pummel and to strike. Samuel again lost consciousness, but the

Gravedigger prevented him from falling and the pounding continued.

John's mind was in turmoil. He had promised Samuel that he would not intervene, but Samuel was now in no state to make any decisions. He was clearly bested and in danger of being permanently hurt.

John threw in the towel, crying repeatedly, "YIELD!" but the howling crowd drowned out his words.

He dived into the ring and grabbed the Gravedigger's arm to stop the incessant blows. The Gravedigger's seconds then joined the furore and punches now rained down on John for his trouble, but he had achieved his objective.

The referee turned to John and enquired, "Bested?"

John nodded his confirmation in an exaggerated fashion so that there could be no misunderstanding.

The referee raised the Gravedigger's arm in victory, to the booing of the crowd.

Samuel was left for a moment, slumped on the canvas in the opposite corner, unconscious and vulnerable.

John hauled him back to his corner, but was unable to revive him.

The surgeon examined Samuel, with a grave expression on his face. Samuel had been drifting in and out of consciousness for over an hour. He winced as hands again examined his back.

The surgeon muttered, "Good", for it meant that pain was being registered in Samuel's brain.

John leaned over to look into his friend's eyes, and when he saw comprehension there, relief surged through him like an elixir.

"Sammy lad," he said, "you're going to be all right – you'll see."

Samuel responded only with his eyes, but the gesture was enough to acknowledge what John was saying.

"Look, Sammy," John continued, "the Prince of Wales was in the crowd. He's sent his own surgeon to attend to you."

The surgeon came into Samuel's vision, and gestured with a polite nod, but his expression remained severe. He leant over Samuel, placed his thumb over Samuel's eyelids and pulled them up to look at his pupils. He mumbled, "Good" again to himself and then stood upright.

"Mr Allenby," John addressed the surgeon by name, "will he recover?"

"There are no broken bones, Sir. He is breathing freely and his brain is not addled."

"You hear that, Sammy boy," said John. "You'll

be all right in a few days, you'll see."

"I fear not," the surgeon interrupted. "Your man has, in my opinion, suffered severe internal injuries. His lower back is badly inflamed and I fear that his system could collapse."

"What can you do for him, sir? " John looked anxiously at the surgeon.

"I can do nothing, sir. I have no physic for what ails him. I can only prescribe careful nursing. His recovery will be in the hands of God. But he has a strong constitution and with luck and his God on his side, then his system may heal itself, with time."

John looked at the surgeon and then back at Samuel. He did not know what to say or do. The silence was uncomfortable and the surgeon coughed in embarrassment.

"I'll bid you good day then, sirs," he said.

"The Prince has agreed to pick up my fee," he added as an afterthought.

A silence fell on the little anti-room at the Fives Court that was Samuel's dressing room.

John felt helpless – his carefree lifestyle had left him ill-equipped to act responsively or deal with an emergency.

A knock on the door broke the silence and an equerry entered. He bowed slightly.

"The Prince of Wales would convey an audience on Mr Medina," he said.

John grabbed at the interruption like a lifeline.

"You hear that, Sammy boy? The Prince of Wales wants to meet you." Samuel, drowning in a sea of pain, forced a bewildered smile.

Six men now crowded into the small room. They moved aside to enable George, Prince of Wales, to step forward from their midst and approach the wounded man.

A large, rotund man with a reddened complexion, the Prince had an affable and jolly countenance.

John stood to attention and bowed with military precision while at the same time introducing himself as Captain John Campbell-John, Samuel Medina's manager and friend. The Prince acknowledged him gracefully, but his attention was focused on Samuel.

He bent over him and smiled. Samuel struggled to rise, but the Prince put his hand on his shoulder to stop him.

"Mr Samuel Medina – and how is it with you, sir?" said the prince politely.

"Very bad, Your Highness, very bad," Samuel answered , through waves of almost overwhelming agony.

"Aye sir, I saw what happened," said the Prince, "and it's a rum do – a rum do indeed."

"Aye, a rum do indeed, sir," winced Samuel, repeating the prince's words. Weakly he attempted a smile, "I fear my opponent has shown he possesses a cloven hoof."

"Agreed, sir," said the prince, "his actions were base in the extreme. There was no doubt in my mind that you were the better man. Your defeat was the result of the basest skullduggery."

"It is a comfort to hear you say so, Your Highness. Thank you, sir."

"Nonsense, sir," said the prince, "it is only the truth and plain for all to see."

"Your servant, sir," Samuel coughed on a gasp of pain.

"Now, Samuel Medina," said the prince, "I have seen your last three fights and they have given me great sport, and what is more, they have swelled my purse, for I have wagered on you."

"I'm sorry to have let you down today, sir."

"Fiddle-de-de," the prince flapped his hand to wave away the apology. "I haven't come here for that. I've come to tell you that I admire the way you fight, sir, and I want to see you fight this Gravedigger fellow again, and show that you are the better man."

"I would like nothing better, Your Highness," said Samuel, "but I fear it will be some time before I am able to fight again."

"Tut-tut," said the prince, "you are a fighter, sir, and may I say, a damned fine one with an uncommon instance of spirit. I've seen you, and you embody all that is good in the British character. I'm sure that you will fight again when your wounds have healed."

Samuel smiled – all that pain would allow.

The Prince patted him on the shoulder regally, then turned and was ushered out of the room by his entourage. The meeting had been brief and its end seemed as sudden as its beginning.

Silence fell again and John forced a smile to reassure Samuel.

"How about that, Sammy," he said encouragingly. "The Prince of Wales himself is an admirer of yours!"

Samuel did not respond. He lay back with

a grimace of pain and contemplated the ceiling.

"It's God's punishment," he said quietly after

a moment's reflection, "for fighting on the Sabbath.

I have displeased my God."

He groped in mid-air, searching for John's arm,

and grasped it. "Send for my father," he whispered.

"Aye, Sammy lad," said John, relieved. "Your own

people will look after you best."

CHAPTER 16   Rebecca

It had been almost a year since his fight with the Gravedigger. Samuel had recovered, but that recovery had been in doubt for quite some time.

His kidneys had ceased to function properly. His face, his joints and his abdomen all swelled, making his appearance grotesque. He spent many weeks vomiting, whilst his head pounded to the rhythm of his heartbeat.

It had taken ten weeks before he was able to leave his sick bed. His doctor could do little, other than prescribe a medicine to keep his temperature down and give his body time to heal itself.

He lost almost three stones in weight as his body's own recuperative powers plundered his reserves of strength and energy, until finally his recovery began. His physical fitness and his youth were the only reasons that he survived.

The papers had been full of that fight and they had been clearly on his side, agreeing with the public that he had been severely wronged. The letters pages had been full of eyewitness accounts of the fight, and there was a clamour for a rematch.

John had been a regular visitor. He had become increasingly agitated and finally confessed to Samuel the extent of his debt. He had amassed a small fortune, but this had all been frittered away by high-living and gambling, and his silver tongue was now unable to keep his creditors at bay.

Samuel loaned him enough to at least pay off his gambling debts, which being a matter of honour were regarded as the most important. His wine merchant, his

tailor and other traders would have to wait.

There was a need to start earning once more.

However, the past year had given Samuel time to

reflect on the dangers he had faced and he was in no

hurry to fight the Bristol Bonecrusher again.

And there was now another and much greater

influence on him. His parents had sent for a second

cousin of his, a Jewish girl by the name of Rebecca, to

nurse him through his illness. At twenty-two she was

the same age as Samuel and well educated.

As well as nursing him, she filled his mind with

poetry. They read and wrote it together, and over the

months he became smitten with her.

Rebecca was diminutive but handsome. She was

one of those people who speaks with their eyes, which

were strikingly large and black and flashed to convey

her emotions.

Rebecca had been his constant companion for almost a year now and they had developed a close relationship. She was the extent of his world and he thought very little about fighting. In fact, fighting was something of which she strongly disapproved.

Rebecca accepted a proposal of marriage from Samuel, after he promised that he would give up fighting.

With one proviso, however – that he had to meet the Bristol Bonecrusher once more. So, almost a year after that horrendous fight, and after a quiet Jewish marriage ceremony, the happy couple moved into a fashionable town house, which was to be their family home.

This, of course, needed money, and it was agreed with Rebecca that Samuel would set up an academy of boxing where he would teach the young gentry the noble science of self-defence.

The academy boomed. It was filled with young gentlemen keen to learn Samuel's new fighting skills. He shamelessly traded on his reputation but, more importantly, that the Prince of Wales himself was an admirer – indeed, he was Samuel's patron.

Over the next few months Samuel gave daily tutorials, sparred with his young gentlemen clients and gave exhibitions of his skills. This was in itself good training, and gradually his fitness returned.

The Academy was a resounding success, and the exhibitions he gave went some way to satisfying the need within him to be a showman.

There was still a clamour from the general public for that rematch with the Gravedigger. At the end of every exhibition everyone wanted to know when that fight was to happen. John Campbell-John was courted by showmen eager to promote the fight because they could all see the prospect for profit.

Articles were written, and speculation was rife but Samuel would fight the Gravedigger when he was ready and not before.

When his mind was made up, Samuel called for John Campbell-John, but he rejected all the offers that had been made. He wanted to promote his own fight – or rather he wanted John to promote it for him.

After an initial shock at this suggestion, John could see the benefit of such an arrangement. The potential returns would be serious money.

Of course, they had to get the Gravedigger to agree to this. They offered him, win or lose, ten percent of the gate in addition to a generous fee. He readily agreed.

Samuel was to get ninety percent of the gate. The venue was to be Marylebone Fields and all who attended were required to pay an entrance fee.

The fight was set for 14th July 1789 at two o'clock. The ticket prices were set much higher than for other big fights but they sold like hot cakes.

Dozens of itinerant workers were hired to erect the stage, set out the seats, and police the perimeter of the Fields and the entrances so that nobody could attend without a ticket.

A whole week before the fight they had enough gate receipts to be sure of a runaway financial success. They also had the prospect of more than doubling that with the standing spectators, who would pay at the gate on the day.

Samuel's recovery was complete. He had built up his body and his stamina, and the sparring he had done had sharpened his reflexes. He was back to his fighting best. In fact he was probably in better shape than when he last met the Gravedigger.

A box at Drury Lane Theatre cost five shillings, so John set equivalent seat prices, with the front two rows paying seven shillings and sixpence.

Standing spectators were charged two shillings and sixpence. Even those meanly clad spectators at the back, who would normally have watched for nothing, were charged a shilling.

One hour before the fight virtually all the seats had been taken and the front standing area was thronged with spectators, tightly packed and bustling with a mix of speculation and anticipation. Bets were being laid with each other and the bookmakers.

There was a great crescendo of noise, building minute by minute.

The crowd was several thousand strong, much to the delighted disbelief of John Campbell-John, who stood on the stage marvelling. Their clamour was music to his ears. He could see all his debts being satisfied from the takings.

When the two contestants emerged, a great roar went up.

John was to be the Master of Ceremonies and had therefore given up his position as Samuel's second to Solomon, Samuel's brother. Big Charles Sweep had been persuaded to act as referee.

The crowd was clearly massively in favour of Samuel, confirming what the newspapers had been saying. They cheered wildly at the barked introduction – 'Samuel the Jew, The Light of Israel' – and he responded with his usual bout of shadow boxing and saluting with his raised arm.

The Gravedigger was applauded with respect from a knowledgeable crowd, but clearly he was not their favourite and his reputation had been tarnished by the foul way in which he had bested Samuel in their previous fight.

The bell sounded thunderously, its custodian intent on not being drowned out by the throng. The bell unleashed a resounding cheer from the crowd and the noise levels rose in expectation.

Samuel instantly took up his normal fighting attitude, as did the Gravedigger, but unlike the first fight he was intent on saving his energy for a lengthy fight and did not rush in.

As before, the Gravedigger's brilliant red hair and pale, freckled, scarred complexion was in stark contrast to Samuel's smooth, olive skin with no hint of damage.

Samuel's raven hair was, as usual, worn long and he had once again entered the ring with it tied at the nape of his neck, much to the displeasure of John who was all too aware of the danger.

Samuel flicked out punches into his opponent's pockmarked face, but each time he did so, the Grave-digger merely took the punch and then sidestepped to cut off Samuel's retreat, trying to force him into a corner from which there was no escape.

After five minutes both men had done little damage. Samuel was briefly backed into a corner but instead of throwing a punch, the Gravedigger lunged at the pigtail at the nape of his neck. Samuel side-stepped quickly, but his opponent had come close to grabbing him by the hair as he had in their first fight.

Watching from the side of the stage, John and Solomon winced with anxiety when they realised the Gravedigger's strategy.

But Samuel had his own strategy. He had relived that first fight endlessly in his mind, going over what he had done right or wrong. He knew his opponent would stalk him, but the danger would diminish as the fight went on.

Samuel had the advantage of speed and agility, but he needed stamina to keep that advantage. His training had been with that in mind.

He now danced around the ring with the nimbleness of a young gazelle, flicking out his bare fist, and soon the blood started to flow until the Gravedigger's face vied with his hair for ownership of the colour red.

Sixteen minutes into the fight Samuel saw the first signs of fatigue in his opponent, who started to blow heavily. This was the signal for the second part of Samuel's strategy. He manoeuvred himself into the centre of the ring where he planted his feet firmly.

He flicked out a stinging left jab into the oncoming face, but followed it up with a powerful right hook that went around the Gravedigger's defence. As the punch landed, Samuel twisted his arm to make it rigid, with all the weight of his half-pivoted body behind it.

The man staggered back in surprise at the severity of the blow, but he smiled perceptibly to see that Samuel was standing his ground and came thundering back.

He threw a mighty left hook followed by a similar right, but Samuel parried the first on his right forearm and then swayed backwards so that the right fell short.

The power of that missed blow put his opponent off balance and wide open for a counter punch. Samuel's right hand came down in an arc, hitting his opponent on the side of the head and the Gravedigger dropped to the canvas.

The crowd roared in appreciation as Samuel looked down at the expression on the Gravedigger's face, which was not so much distress as disbelief.

Dazed, he jumped to his feet, but Big Charles Sweep stepped in between the two fighters, and signalled for the bell, that duly sounded.

Samuel went back to his corner, turned and looked back at the Gravedigger in the opposite corner. His confidence paramount, Samuel grinned and said:

"I'll best him within thirty minutes."

                                  A Pair of Scissors

Solomon, however, was not listening. Seizing the opportunity, whilst Samuel was concentrating his attention on his opponent, he produced a pair of scissors and calmly cut off his brother's pigtail.

Teeth bared, Samuel turned angrily and grabbed Solomon by the collar. His brother held up the palms of his hands, one still holding the scissors and the other a tail of raven hair.

"Forgive me, brother, but the Gravedigger will have you by the hair just like he did the last time. We must deny him that advantage."

The bell sounded again. The Gravedigger had obtained a brief respite from the thirty second break, and Samuel should have danced until its effects had drained from his opponent's legs.

But he was still angry at what his brother had done, and he stood his ground in the centre of the ring.

He parried two more round punches and then followed up with a muscular uppercut that ripped through his opponent's guard. The contact launched a cocktail of blood and mucus into the air, spattering the resplendent clothes of Big Charles Sweep.

The Gravedigger took the blow without a backwards step and lunged at Samuel, reaching round the back of his head to the nape of his neck, but grabbing at thin air.

Samuel, alarmed, stepped backwards and immediately realised that, thanks to his brother's foresight, he had had a narrow escape.

With that, his anger ebbed away. His calculating, fighting mind now reasserted itself and he returned to his strategy.

He danced for five more minutes, but then began to stop and parry, his own heavy punches starting to hit home.

Each time a powerful blow landed the crowd roared. Very soon Samuel was able to hit his opponent at will and the contest took on the appearance of an exhibition fight.

The Gravedigger's face was a mess – his flesh mashed by Samuel's bare knuckles. Blood was smeared across his features so that he wore a vermilion mask. His right eye was already closed and his left was closing fast so he could no longer see the punches coming.

Samuel now played his matador role and walked up and down before his bested foe, flicking out left jabs that provoked his opponent to throw wild punches in response, but with his vision so badly restricted the only thing he had left was his bravery.

But Samuel had a score to settle. To this point his mind had been calculating and his approach totally professional.

He was not by nature a vindictive man, but the Gravedigger had wronged him grievously. He began to taunt him. He moved his weight to his right and sank a potent, gut-wrenching blow under the Gravedigger's ribcage, but he did not retreat out of danger. His opponent doubled up in pain and Samuel heard the air rip from his lungs.

Samuel leaned over, hissed, "Is this all you've chuffing well got?" and then sent another penetrating blow into the vulnerable man's midriff.

"Where's your blasted cheating now, eh?" Samuel crowed as another punch beat into the bent figure. "You need to be taught a damned good lesson, my man."

Before he walked away he launched a final punch,

accompanied by the single word "BASTARD!" which

seemed to enhance the power of it.

Samuel raised his right hand high into the air to

signal to the crowd that the matador was going to

dispatch the bull and the crowd responded with

a collective "HUZZAH!"

The blow came crashing down. The Gravedigger

wobbled but his courage kept him upright. His guard

returned as a reflex action, but there was little actual

protection from it.

Samuel's right hand rose high into the sky again,

and again the crowd bayed – "HUZZAH!" The blow came

swooping down like a hawk homing in on its prey.

It hit home cruelly and the man staggered

backwards and then fell back hitting his head on the

canvas as he did so. The bell sounded and he was

carried unconscious back to his corner.

His seconds tried feverishly to revive their man. Water was poured over him and then smelling salts were waved before his nostrils but his nasal passages were too full of blood for any vapour to penetrate.

After thirty seconds they heaved the Gravedigger to his feet, but those few flickering dregs of consciousness that had briefly surfaced had now evaporated again. His legs were dysfunctional, his head flopped downwards, his mouth gaped wide open and his chin rested firmly on his chest.

The only sign of vital activity was the gargled breathing emanating from his powerful lungs.

Nevertheless, the seconds dragged their man to the centre of the ring in some deluded hope that he could fight on. They released him, but he simply crumpled and fell to the floor.

The fight was over and Charles Sweep held the victor's arm.

A shout of adulation went up and gentlemen threw their tall hats into the air.

Samuel bathed in the crowd's adoration, strutting about the ring both arms raised high in triumph. He visited each corner so that the whole crowd could see him and he could see them.

He had proved himself to be the governor, but he had proved much more than that.

He had proved he was a fighting man of unparalleled skill, but more importantly, he had proved to be a noble hero; one who had shown that the little man can prevail against the bully. Samuel was indeed their hero.

John took to the centre of the ring to announce to the crowd the result of the battle. It was a superfluous action but it was part of the show, part of the spectacle.

He barked out an obvious statement, raising Samuel's hand again as he did so.

"The winner – Samuel the Jew – 'The Light of Israel'."

The crowd rose to give their hero a standing ovation, for they knew they had seen something special.

Samuel responded to the adulation once again.

Samuel Medina was a pugilist of immense proficiency, a man of honour, a handsome man and a showman, but when the euphoria of the moment was over, he was still just a man.

In the coming years he would have more battles to fight, but not all would be in the ring. Treachery would be a far more dangerous opponent.

Characters in the story:

Samuel Medina	a champion fist fighter
John Campbell-John	Samuel's friend and manager
Charles Sweep	a fighter and referee
Norbert Openshaw	a fighter who competes as "The Lancashire Soldier"
Irish Michael the Carrier	a fighter
Sir Thomas Kettall	Samuel's sponsor
Daniel the Gravedigger	a fighter who competes as "The Bristol Bonecrusher"
Mr Allenby	a surgeon
The Prince of Wales	eldest son of the king
Rebecca	Samuel's second cousin, then his wife
Soloman	Samuel's brother

Word meanings:

Aquiline	hooked
Bayed	howled like dogs
Buoy	floating marker
Cloven hoof	a sign of the devil
Creditable	believable
Custodian	person in charge
Diminutive	very small
Discomfited	embarrassed
Doffed	took off
Dour	po-faced
Dunderhead	fool
Elixir	strong medicine
Embezzlement	stealing money entrusted to you
Evasively	avoiding the truth
Farthings	coins of very little value
Fives	a sport like squash
Float	starting fund of money
Fracas	scuffle, disturbance
Frittered away	wasted
Furore	row, shouting
Guinea	21 shillings
Huzzah	hurrah
Impartially	fairly

Impromptu	unplanned
Matador	bull fighter
Naïve	too trusting
Nubbins	contributions of money
Paradoxically	strangely
Persona	character
Physique	body
Pugilist	fighter
Prestigious	high status
Proficiency	skill
Proviso	condition
Quintessential	perfect
Recuperative	getting better
Retribution	repayment
Sabbath	day of worship
Scallywag	disreputable person
Sedan chair	method of transport for rich people
Shako	soldier's uniform peaked cap
Skullduggery	cheating
Sovereign	20 shillings
Superfluous	unnecessary
Unorthodox	unusual

FIST FIGHTER: CODE OF HONOUR is an excerpt

from a much longer novel by Stephen Taylor,

entitled NO QUARTER ASKED, NO QUARTER GIVEN,

published in 2008

ISBN 0-9552315-3-1 / 978-0-9552315-3-7

www.ingramcontent.com/pod-product-compliance
Lightning Source LLC
Chambersburg PA
CBHW032048180726
48284CB00004B/1231